Mattie AND THE Chicken Thief

IDA LUTTRELL

Mattie
AND THE
Chicken Thief

ILLUSTRATED BY THACHER HURD

DODD, MEAD & COMPANY
New York

Published by Dodd, Mead & Company, Inc.,
71 Fifth Avenue, New York, N.Y. 10003

Printed in the United States of America by Horowitz/Rae

Designed by Barbara DuPree Knowles

1 2 3 4 5 6 7 8 9 10

Library of Congress Cataloging-in-Publication Data
Luttrell, Ida.
Mattie and the chicken thief.
Summary: When Prowler the cat and Howler the dog
accidentally scare their mistress's precious chickens
into the woods, she prepares to catch an imaginary thief
while they try to get the chickens back.
[1. Cats—Fiction. 2. Dogs—Fiction. 3. Chickens—
Fiction] I. Hurd, Thacher, ill. II. Title.
PZ7.L97953Mat 1988   [E]   87-24451
ISBN 0-396-09126-1

*To my son, Billy, who knows
all about Mattie*—IL

*For Emily and Jonathan
and Prowler*—TH

Mattie had a cat named Prowler, a dog named Howler,
and four hens, Dusty, Rusty, Ruffles, and Pearl. They
all lived together in a little white house by the woods—
except for the chickens who lived in a hen house out back.

"Pretty little hens," Mattie said as she threw grain to her chickens, "I feed you and you feed me." And that was true because each day the hens laid four brown eggs.

Mattie cooked two eggs and saved two eggs to trade at the store for a little meat and milk. So Mattie and Prowler and Howler were never hungry.

Once, when the moon was full
and the night too bright for
sleeping, Howler and Prowler
went on a romp. But Prowler
stumbled, tripping Howler.
Yipping and yowling, Howler
chased Prowler across the yard
and through the hen house.

"Woollybangers!" the terrified hens squawked, as they jumped off their roost and fled to the woods.

The noise woke Mattie. She
grabbed her lantern and ran
to the hen house.

"A thief took my chickens!"
she cried as she saw the empty
roost. "We will all starve!"

Howler and Prowler flopped
at her feet, their tongues
hanging out.

"Bless you," she said, "you
tried to catch that thief."

Howler pretended to look
for fleas between his toes.

Prowler nudged Howler and
whispered, "What did she say?"

"We will starve," said Howler.

"Hush that barking," Mattie
said. "A body can't think! I'm
figuring a way to get my hens."

She stomped to the kitchen muttering, "A chicken thief always comes back. I aim to catch this one."

Howler and Prowler waited by the hen house.

"Now what?" Prowler said.

"We go after the hens," said Howler.

"Now?" asked Prowler.

"Not yet," said Howler.

Mattie returned with a ball of old twine, pots and pans, and a cornhusk chicken. She set the fake chicken on the roost. Then she strung the twine back and forth, up and down, in and out, over and around from the hen house to the porch. She tied the pots and pans right in the middle.

"Come on, Howler and Prowler," Mattie said. "Wait by the kitchen and watch for the thief. Wake me when he comes."

"What did she say?" asked Prowler.

"Wait," said Howler.

Mattie blew out the light and went to bed.

"Now!" said Howler, and he and Prowler started for the woods. But Prowler blundered into the maze. The twine broke and tangled around her. Prowler yowled and crashed through the trees, the pots and pans clattering behind her.

"Stop!" Howler cried.

Dusty, Rusty, Ruffles, and
Pearl heard them coming.
"Woollybangers again!"
they all screamed as they
darted deeper into the woods.
The pots and pans caught
on a bush and Prowler leaped
free. Shaky and tired, she
headed home. Howler was at
her heels crying, "Don't quit now!"

Mattie met them with her lantern. "That worthless thief got away and took my pots and pans to boot. Next time he'll make off with my dog and cat."

So she put Howler and Prowler in the kitchen and latched the screen door. Mattie shook her fist at the night. "I'll show that thief," she said. "I will build a better trap. This time I mean business."

The next morning Mattie went to work with bells and strings and old bed springs while Howler and Prowler watched from inside the kitchen. Mattie hammered crates and cans and rusty fans and nailed them to her thief trap. Days went by as Mattie tied wire and wheels to gears that squealed . . . and the trap became bigger and bigger.

While she worked, Dusty, Rusty, Ruffles, and Pearl
made a new home in the woods. They slept in the trees
at night and ate seeds and berries and bugs all day.

Prowler and Howler grew hungry and worried by
the latched kitchen door.

Finally, after much banging and clanging and old wire whanging, Mattie finished her trap. She pushed and pulled it to the empty hen house.

"*There*!" she said. "This trap had better catch that thief tonight because my cupboard is mighty bare!" Then Mattie went to bed without any supper.

Their growling stomachs kept Howler and Prowler awake.

"Oh, for a little meat," Howler said, and he tried to nose the door open.

"Milk and cheese," Prowler whined.

"Hush in there!" Mattie said. "A body can't sleep. Besides, you'll scare off the thief."

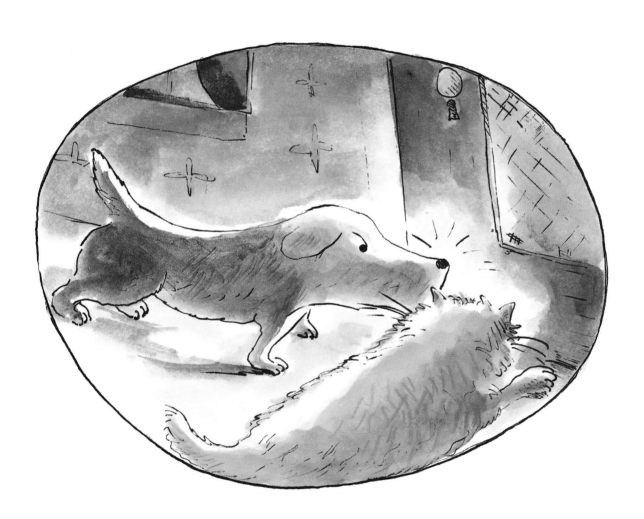

Howler pushed harder against the door. The latch held fast but the screen popped loose.

"Out!" he cried, and Howler and Prowler were off.

They dashed to the woods where they found Dusty,
Rusty, Ruffles, and Pearl asleep in a tree.

"You go up," said Howler. "I'll stay down."

In a flurry of scratching claws and flying
bark, Prowler scrambled up the tree.

Dusty, Rusty, Ruffles, and
Pearl burst into action.
Wings flapped, beaks snapped,
and flying feet beat the air.
    "Help!" they screeched.
"It's those woollybangers *again*!"
And they flew off in all
directions.

BONK!

"This way!" Howler roared. He and Prowler chased
and circled the hens and herded them down the path
to the hen house.

Blind with fear, the hens threw themselves into
the trap. Bells rang, wires sang, gears and cans
and rusty fans all made a terrible racket.

Mattie jumped out of bed. "The thief!" she cried,
and she ran to the hen house.

"Oh, happy day!" she said. "My pretty little hens are home. But I am not a bit surprised. That thief knew I meant business!"

"What did she say?" asked Prowler.
"Never mind," said Howler . . .

"Tonight we eat!"